YPC/PC

Night, Light, Sleep Tight

For Fiona, with love ~
JB
For Olive and Joseph, with love ~
RB

First published in 2010 by Scholastic Children's Books
Euston House, 24 Eversholt Street
London NW1 1DB
a division of Scholastic Ltd
www.scholastic.com
London ~ New York ~ Toronto ~ Sydney ~ Auckland
Mexico City ~ New Delhi ~ Hong Kong

Text copyright © 2010 Janet Bingham
Illustrations copyright © 2010 Rosalind Beardshaw

HB ISBN 978 1407 11037 0
PB ISBN 978 1407 11038 7

Night, Light, Sleep Tight

Written by
Janet Bingham

Illustrated by
Rosalind Beardshaw

SCHOLASTIC

Jack was trying to fall asleep.
He closed one eye and then the other.
He put his head under his wing, and took it out again.
Nothing worked.

The night was dark, and Jack was scared of the dark.
"Oh, dear!" he sighed. "Night-time is so dark and scary.
I wish it was light-time!"

"Yoo-hoo!" hooted a merry voice.

Jack jumped. "Who's there?" he quacked.
"It's me, Olivia," said a very small owl.

"Shouldn't you be asleep?" said Jack.
"Not me!" hooted Olivia. "My family sleep in
the light-time. Do you want to play with me?"

"I will in the morning," said Jack.
"But I'm trying to go to sleep now."

"Then I'll help!" said Olivia. "I'll sing you to sleep."
She hooted a gentle lullaby.

Very soon Jack's eyes began to close, and he fell fast asleep.

When Jack woke up, it was starting to get light.
"Hello," whispered Olivia. But she didn't sound cheerful now.
"What's the matter?" quacked Jack.

"I'm scared," said Olivia. "I've never been out in the light-time before. Everything looks different. And the hot sun is coming!"

"There's no need to be afraid of the sun," said Jack.
The sky was turning pink and gold.
"Oooh!" said Olivia. "It's pretty!"

"Don't look right at the sun – it
might hurt your eyes. But it feels
nice on your feathers," said Jack,
as the sun appeared.

"It's not too hot after all," said Olivia. "And look at all the bright colours everywhere!"
"Come on," said Jack. "There's lots to see in the light-time!"

Jack led the way up the path and Olivia
followed. Suddenly she cried, "Ooh, ooh!
There's something stuck to my feet!"

"That's your shadow-shape," explained
Jack. "Look! You can make it small,
like an egg… or tall…"
"… like a grown-up!" giggled Olivia.
"See how big we are? Let's race!"

And off they ran, chasing their shadows in the sunshine.

Later on, Jack went swimming. Olivia watched him ducking and bobbing on the pond.

She dipped a toe in the water.

"I wish I could swim," she said.

"I wish *I* could climb trees!" laughed Jack.

Just then, a flock of geese flew overhead.

"Imagine…" whispered Jack.
"…one day…" sighed Olivia.
"…we'll be able to fly!"

At last Olivia yawned.
"I'm ready to go to sleep now," she said.

A blackbird was singing nearby.
"Let's join in!" said Jack, and they hooted
and quacked all the way home.

Back at her nest, Olivia started
to hop up to bed.
"Light, light," she murmured, sleepily.
"Light, light," replied Jack. "Sleep tight!"

That evening Jack stayed awake and watched
the sun set. Olivia came out of her nest.
She scooted down through the branches.

"Yoo hoo," she hooted.
But Jack looked worried.
"What's the matter?"
asked Olivia.

"I'm still a little bit scared," said Jack.
"The sun has gone, and it's getting cold and dark!"

"There's no need to be afraid of the dark," said Olivia.
"Come and see the moon."

Olivia stayed with Jack as the moon came up.
They watched it brighten. The stars began to sparkle.
Fireflies danced over the moonlit water.
 "I didn't know the night-time was full
of lights," said Jack.

"Look at the shapes in the stars," said Olivia.
"There's a duck!"
"And there's an owl!" laughed Jack.

After a while Jack started to yawn.
"I'm ready to go to sleep now," he said.

Jack snuggled down in his nest.
"Thank you for showing me
the moon," he said. "I'm not
frightened of the night-time any more."

"And I'm not frightened of the light-time," said Olivia.
"Thank you for being my friend."

"Light, night," said Jack, with a sleepy smile.
"Night, light…" laughed Olivia.

"Sleep tight."

The End